T0146871

A Wave of Love

A TRUE LOVE STORY

Julia McGregor

BALBOA.PRESS

A DIVISION OF HAY HOUSE

Balboa Press books may be ordered through booksellers or by contacting:

Balboa Press
A Division of Hay House
1663 Liberty Drive
Bloomington, IN 47403
www.balboapress.com.au
1 (877) 407-4847

Because of the dynamic nature of the Internet, any web addresses or links contained in this book may have changed since publication and may no longer be valid. The views expressed in this work are solely those of the author and do not necessarily reflect the views of the publisher, and the publisher hereby disclaims any responsibility for them.

The author of this book does not dispense medical advice or prescribe the use of any technique as a form of treatment for physical, emotional, or medical problems without the advice of a physician, either directly or indirectly. The intent of the author is only to offer information of a general nature to help you in your quest for emotional and spiritual well-being. In the event you use any of the information in this book for yourself, which is your constitutional right, the author and the publisher assume no responsibility for your actions.

Any people depicted in stock imagery provided by Getty Images are models, and such images are being used for illustrative purposes only. Certain stock imagery © Getty Images.

Print information available on the last page.

ISBN: 978-1-5043-2148-8 (sc)
ISBN: 978-1-5043-2149-5 (e)

Balboa Press rev. date: 04/22/2020

Contents

Chapter 1

T he air was filled with the slight smell of plane fuel. Sydney airport was packed with what seemed like a million people. Newly graduated marine biologist Emma Smith was on her way to her dream job. She had been selected to work and live on Heron Island. She looked down at her plane ticket to Airlie beach and smiled. Her life was finally coming together. She grasped her suitcase and headed towards the departure sign. Emma checked in her luggage and walked over to her gate, holding the straps of her bag. She walked through staring at her plane. As soon as the clock stroked 3 pm she would depart from Sydney forever. She glanced at the clock. 2:45 pm. She casually walked over to the window and looked out onto the runway. She watched the planes land and take off. Her phone buzzed; it was now 3 pm. She walked over to the gate, clutching onto her plane ticket as her life depended on it. She showed her ticket and walked out the door onto the runway. She was blasted with the smell of plane fuel and a rush of excitement. There on the runway were people in Fluro vests directing her, and the other passengers to the back of the plane. She climbed up the stairs and boarded the plane. She found her seat towards the back. It was the window seat. She smiled as she looked out the window, not realising her hands were shaking.

"Nervous flyer, are you?" asked the man seated next to her.

Emma looked over at him and sat there frozen. Her eyes opened widely and her heart began to race. Who was this man and how was he so good looking? He had beautiful tanned skin, brown hair and hazel eyes. She easily got lost in them before she was dragged back to reality.

"Ehh no, just excited" she stuttered, "um, I am Emma Smith".

Emma put out her hand and the man shook it gently.

"Liam Jones" he replied smiling. "So, Emma, what is taking you to Airlie Beach" he continued.

"I am going to work. I got a job on Heron Island as a marine biologist but mainly in conservation" Emma answered.

"Wow that's amazing and a complete coincidence because I got a job for the same role," said Liam smiling widely.

As Emma was about to reply she was interrupted by the piolet over the speaker. As she watched the flight attendant's instructions, Liam gazed at sunlight catching her face. How could someone be so beautiful? She turned her head and he quickly turned his head away. Emma gave a small chuckle and looked back out the window. This was going to be the best two-hour flight of her life.

The pilot stopped talking and the seatbelt light turned on. Emma clipped in and was almost immediately pushed back into her seat. She felt the plane take off into the air. She looked out the window and watched the distant boats and waves in Sydney Harbour.

"It's amazing how the ocean can brighten up a city," said Liam.

Emma looked over at him.

"Not a city person?" she asked.

"Nah, I grew up in Foster. I remember I used to surf about three times a day before I had to move down to the city. It was horrible but I am overwhelmed that I got this job away from all that city vibe. What about you?" asked Liam.

"I grew up in Newcastle all my life" replied Emma, "But I never loved it. I have always loved the beach with a passion. I just want to save it, it's just too amazing to let it go".

"I feel the same way," said Liam, staring into Emma's eyes.

Emma smiled slightly. Their moment was suddenly disrupted by the plane jolting downwards. Emma grasped Liam's hand. The plane stabilised, it was just turbulence. Emma's and Liam's eyes both stared at their hand's interwind. Emma pulled her hand away quickly.

"Sorry about that," said Emma.

"No, it's totally fine" Liam replied smiling.

The hours seemed like minutes as the seatbelt light

was once again turned on. The plane started to descend into the tropics of Queensland. As the plane touched the runway, Emma let out a little squeal of excitement. Emma and Liam waited for everyone to leave the plane before they got up. Emma left the plane and took in the view. The sky was pale blue and the runway was surrounded by palm trees. As Emma was walking on the runway, she felt a hand lightly grab her arm. She turned around and it was Liam. He leaned close to her and whispered something in her ear.

"By the way, if you were wondering, I'm single" whispered Liam.

Before she could say anything, Liam was too far away. She looked at her hand and saw a small piece of paper. As she opened it her face glowed up. It was his phone number. Emma put the paper in her jean pockets and walked into the airport. She grabbed her suitcase and headed towards to boat to Heron Island that was waiting for her. She sat down watching the ocean waves crash against the side of the boat. The ocean was glittering like a thousand diamonds in the sunlight. The boat came to a stop as it reached the jetty of Heron Island. The piers of the jetty were covered in small barnacles. She smiled as she walked down the jetty. There at the end was a woman holding a sign with her name on it and next to her a man holding a sign with Liam's name on it. Her heart fluted.

"Follow me Emma," said the woman politely. Emma followed her onto the island.

Chapter 2

Emma walked into her small house and gasped. It was small but beautiful. All of her items from her home in Newcastle had arrived. She started work in two days. She instantly started to unpack. There was a small knock on the door. It was from Liam!

"Hey stranger," said Liam laughing.

"Hey Liam, what are you doing here," asked Emma.

"Well, we are neighbours so I decided to do the neighbourly thing and come and say hi" explained Liam.

"Yeah sure thing" replied Emma smiling.

"You need help unpacking?" asked Liam.

Emma smiled at him and nodded her head. Liam helped Emma unpack all of her things.

"Hey Emma, if you're not doing anything tomorrow night, there is this nice restaurant" started Liam.

Before Liam could finish Emma interrupted him.

"Yes," she squealed.

"I'll pick you up at 7, tomorrow," said Liam.

Liam walked out of her house. Emma smiled. She had not been with someone for what seemed like years. Emma continued to unpack her luggage and items from storage. She could not stop smiling. Then she realised, tomorrow was also orientation before her first day. With the help Liam had given her, Emma was fully unpacked. She grabbed her keys and purse and headed over too

Baillie's Bar (the bar on Heron Island). When Emma arrived, she sat up at the bar.

"Hello Ms, what can I get for you?" asked the bartender.

Emma grabbed the drink menu.

"I'll have the Mai Tai cocktail please" she replied.

A few moments past and the bartender gave her the drink. She took her drink over to a table overlooking the ocean. The view was beautiful. As the sun started to set, the sky turned bright orange. Despite the noise of the bar, it was quiet. The waves brushed up onto the sand washing bits of broken coral onto the shore. Emma finished her drink, paid, and took a sunset walk on the jetty. As she walked over to the jetty, the sand was soft against her feet. The sun had now nearly fully set as Emma finished walking to the end of the jetty. Her legs dangling off the sides. She looked down into the crystal-clear water amazed. A meter below her was a beautiful Manta ray, peacefully swimming in the small tide. It swam so carelessly. Emma watched as it disappeared into the reef out into the ocean. The sun had now fully set. She looked up and placed her hand over her mouth. She had never seen so many stars. There were millions. Emma pushed herself up and walked home in the moonlight ready for the day ahead.

The sun pushed through the soft silk curtains of Emma's room. She slowly woke to look out her window. The view was truly a blessing. She looked out into the vastness of the ocean, smiling. Emma pushed herself out of bed and changed. It was orientation. She quickly made her way over to the research station grabbing a banana on her way out. She arrived an hour early. She sat outside and sighed. What was she going to do for an hour? She then heard someone calling her name out from behind her. It was Liam's voice.

"Oh, hey Liam," said Emma. "What are you doing here so early?"

"I could ask you the same thing" replied Liam.

He gave a cheeky smile as he sat down next to her.

"Excited to start work?" asked Liam.

Emma looked over at Liam and rolled her eyes.

"Is that even a question?" asked Emma. "Of course, I am. I have my absolute dream job, especially as I am working with the turtle hatchery conservation department. What are you working on?"

"Ok this is crazy but the same department as you" replied Liam.

Emma looked at him shocked. How on earth was she going to be able to work with him around her, especially after tonight. As she started to reply she was interrupted by her boss.

"Ah you must be Emma and Liam" started Sam, the head researcher. "Welcome to Heron Island. Today is

11

about getting to know your way around the island and our research facility. So, if you two could follow me."

Emma and Liam followed Sam through the glass doors of the research facility and were amazed. It was truly amazing. They continued to follow Sam into their department. Inside, were multiple turtle egg incubators and a large glass window overlooking the vast ocean. It was pure beauty. Sam led them to two small rooms.

"These are your offices. This is where you will come tomorrow when you start tomorrow morning" explained Sam. "I will see you both tomorrow".

Emma and Liam walked out of the facility. Emma stood still gazing at the view. She could not believe she was here!

"Oh well, I guess I will see you tonight," said Liam.

"Yeah, I cannot wait" replied Emma smiling.

The day seemed to go past quickly and before Emma knew it, it was 6:30 pm. She stared at her closet endlessly. What was she going to wear? She started to go through her closet franticly until she found a small white beach dress. She changed into it, curled her hair and grabbed her purse. She walked out of her door and met Liam outside.

Chapter 3

"Wow, you look gorgeous," said Liam. "Come on let's go!".

Emma and Liam walked to Shearwater restaurant.

"Hi, welcome to Shearwater restaurant" started the administrator. "Do you have a reservation?"

"Yes, two for Jones" replied Liam.

"Ah yes, the ocean view table specifically requested. Tonight's menu is the traditional roast buffet. So, when you are ready to order, pay at the desk and fill up your plate" she explained.

"Thank you" replied Liam as he grabbed Emma's hand.

Her heart started to race. He was holding her hand. She felt shots of electricity go through her body. She had never felt a spark like this before. She did not realise she was standing still. She felt Liam's hand slip away.

"I am sorry, I…" stared Liam.

"No, it fine" replied Emma.

She grabbed his hand and they walked over to their table. Liam quickly walked ahead and pulled out Emma's chair.

"Haha, thank you!" said Emma.

Her face lit up. Liam sat across from her. They watched the sunset whilst they ate. The previous night, the sunset had been orange but tonight was different. The sky was rose pink. The colour of love.

"Hey Emma, would you like to go on a night beach walk?" asked Liam.

"I would love too," replied Emma.

Liam rose from his chair and gently grabbed Emma's hand. They walked out of the restaurant with their fingers interwind. They walked down onto the softness of the sand and sat down.

"So, Liam, what makes you like the ocean so much?" asked Emma.

"I honestly don't know" he replied. "I have grown up around it all my life. I guess you could say it's my second home. What about you?"

"I feel like I have always had a connection to the ocean" Emma started. "I knew this when I went to Hamilton Island back in high school. I was swimming in the reef and I just felt free, that's when I made it my purpose to help conserve the ocean, and also I love turtles hence why I am working with them".

They gazed into each other's eyes. They were perfect for each other. It was like fate had brought them together. Liam started to lean in and Emma closed her eyes. All-time around them stopped. It was just them in that moment. A moment of pure love and happiness. Liam pulled away and smiled.

"That was unexpected" laughed Emma.

Liam looked at her and laughed.

"What?" asked Emma smiling.

"Do you know how red you are currently" laughed Liam.

Emma's smiled faded and she got up.

She felt Liam grab her hand and turned her around.

"Don't worry, I think it's cute" he said smiling.

The sun had completely set and the island was silent. The only sound that could be heard was the tide rushing up against the jetty piers. Liam walked Emma home.

"Well, I guess I will see you tomorrow morning," said Liam.

He leaned in once more as timed stopped. Emma pulled away and whispered in his ear.

"Goodnight".

Emma softly closed her door as he walked away. She changed out of her dress and instantly fell asleep. Her life was finally together.

Chapter 4

The soft buzzing of Emma's alarm clock woke her. It was her first day at her dream job and even better, Liam would be there. Emma jumped out of bed and changed into her work uniform. As she grabbed an apple from her kitchen counter she headed over to her office. When she arrived, Sam was waiting at her desk.

"Hi Sam, how are you?" she asked.

"Listen Emma I hate to do this to you but you don't have enough funds to complete your accommodation payment. So, unless you find a way to live here, we won't be able to keep you. You have two days" explained Sam. "I'm sorry Emma, truly".

Sam walked out of her office. Emma sank to the ground. Her eyes flooded with tears. She knew this was too good to be true. All the sounds around her were drowned out by her sobbing. She did not notice Liam walk in.

As Liam walked in, he noticed Emma on the floor, hunched over, crying.

"Emma sweetie, what's wrong?" asked Liam.

Emma looked up at him, wiping the tears from her face. Her eyes were bright red and tired.

"Oh nothing, its ok" replied Emma.

Liam hugged Emma tightly.

"Well, I know something that will cheer you up" started Liam. "We are going out onto the reef today to count turtle numbers".

"Oh cool" replied Emma.

They both grabbed their gear and walked over to the jetty where the research vessel was waiting. They boarded the boat and sat on the deck, watching the island fade into the distance.

"Alright, gear up" yelled Sam.

Liam helped Emma put on her scuba diving gear. She was about to dive in the reef but she could feel a sense of happiness. She dived into the water and it was amazing. The reef was beautiful. If only she wasn't going home in two days. She closed her eyes and felt the current pulling her out into the sea. She followed. She was one with the ocean. She carelessly swam through the reef taking in its beauty when suddenly a green turtle came from under her. She carefully held onto its shell and swam with it. She could not help herself but smile. She turned her head as a dark shadow approached her. It was from Liam. He held out his hand and she took it. They swam through the reef for what seemed like hours. Liam looked at his watch and pointed up to the surface of the water. It was time to head back to the ship. They swam until they saw the anchor. They both broke through the surface of the water. Liam helped Emma climb onto the boat and remove her scuba gear.

"Thanks," she said vaguely.

Emma reported her turtle sightings to Sam before the boat docked onto the island. As the boat docked at the jetty Emma sprinted off the ship to her house. She pushed the door open and ran straight into her room crying her heart out. Today had been amazing but she would not get to experience again. Her life had come to a stop. Her dream job taken from her. All was lost.

Liam walked into Emma's room and rested his hand on her shoulder.

"Emma, seriously, what's wrong?" asked Liam.

Emma sat up, wrapping her blanket around her and told Liam.

"So basically, I don't have enough money to stay here. And if I don't come up with a solution, I'll be going back to Newcastle in two days" cried Emma.

Liam put his arm around her.

"I have a solution," he said.

Emma looked up at him. Her eyes were full of desperation.

"You could come and live with me?" he asked.

Emma blinked expressionlessly.

"Are you serious?" asked Emma.

Liam wiped the tears off Emma's face.

"Yes," he replied.

He gently kissed her on the cheek.

"I also have a confession to make" began Liam. "I know we have only known each other for three days but I have never felt like this about anyone. I love you, Emma".

Emma's face brightened with the biggest smile Liam had ever witnessed.

"I love you too Liam" replied Emma.

Emma leapt onto Liam wrapping her arms around him. She got out of bed and grabbed her purse.

"Where are you going?" asked Liam.

"Over to see Sam, to tell him that I'm not going anywhere" replied Emma.

Emma skipped out of her house and over to Sam's office.

"Sam" yelled Emma walking into his office. "I have a solution".

"Emma. I am glad to hear it! What is it?" asked Sam.

"I am moving in with Liam," said Emma.

Sam looked at her speechless.

"Don't worry we will be splitting the expenses" continued Emma.

"Wait, you and Liam? Are you guys" started Sam.

"Yes" interrupted Emma. "Anyways, I will see you at work tomorrow morning".

Emma walked out of Sam's office and walked back to her new home. Liam's house. When she arrived home, Liam had already started to move boxes into his house.

"How did it go honey?" he asked.

Emma ran up to him smiling wrapping her arms around him.

"Let's just say, we are officially living together now," said Emma.

Liam pulled away from the hug and kissed her. Emma smiled as they walked into their house.

"I am going to cook you dinner tonight, honey," said Liam.

Emma looked at him and laughed.

"You're going to cook for me?" asked Emma confused.

"Yep" replied Liam

"Ok" answered Emma. "What are you going to cook for me?"

"I am going to cook you gourmet burritos" replied Liam smiling.

An hour past and Liam called Emma to the table. There in front of her was truly a gourmet burrito. She had a bite and looked directly at Liam.

"This tastes amazing!" said Emma.

"I'm glad you like it" replied Liam.

They finished eating, washed up and then went to bed.

"Do you have a particular side?" asked Liam.

"No, I usually sleep in the middle" Emma replied laughing.

They climbed into bed. Liam placed his arms around her. Emma's heart fluttered. This was going to be a sleepless night, but not necessarily a bad thing.

"Love you," said Liam kissing her cheek.

"I love you too" replied Emma smiling.

Emma lent over, turned her light out and closed her eyes. She had never been so happy.

Chapter 5

One Year Later

I t had been a year since Emma and Liam had met on the plane. It had been the best year of both their lives. Today was a very special day. It was their anniversary of when Emma and Liam first met.

The warmth of the sun kissed Emma's tanned skin as she slept peacefully. Liam sat up next to her, watching her sleep. He was lost in her beauty. Emma rolled over and slightly opened her eyes. She saw Liam gazing at her and smiled.

"You know its creepy watching someone sleep," Emma said.

"No honey, it's romantic" chuckled Liam.

Emma pushed herself up next to Liam.

"I remember a year ago, I thought to myself, I cannot wait for the day I wake up next to you" confessed Liam. "And now, my dream has come true".

Liam brushed the hair out of Emma's face and kissed her softly. Emma looked up into his hazel eyes and once again she was lost in them. She was pulled back to reality when she heard his voice.

"So, are we going into work today?" asked Liam.

Emma looked over at the clock.

"Is that the time!" she yelled.

Emma jumped out of bed and frantically changed into her work uniform.

"Are you coming?" asked Emma.

"I have the day off, enjoy work though honey," said Liam.

Emma gave him a quick smile as she ran out of the door. As she arrived at work. Sam was waiting at her desk. Hopefully, this time was good news.

"I just want to say congratulations Emma" Sam said as she walked in.

"Congratulations for what?" asked Emma.

"Well, you see Emma" started Sam. "I am stepping down; I got a job up at Townsville so I need someone to fill the role of head researcher. I have been watching you for the past year and I know you have what it takes. You are driven by passion and your love for the ocean and it is truly inspiring. So, from this moment I am officially promoting you. Congratulations head researcher".

Sam walked out of the room.

Emma closed her office door and squealed with joy. She had more than her dream job. She had the best job she could ever think of.

She looked up as her door opened, it was Sam.

"I forgot to tell you. Starting tomorrow you will be in my office." Sam told her.

Sam walked back out. She was going to be in Sam's office. That thing was massive. Emma grabbed her lab coat off her office door and headed down to the lab. Once she walked all of her workers applauded her. She could not help but smile. As she walked over to her station she was interrupted by a new intern.

"Excuse me, Ms Smith. Can I show you something?" she asked.

"Sure thing. How old are you?" asked Emma. "You seem young".

"My name is Ava and I'm 16. I am here on work experience" she explained.

"Well Ava, not many people get to complete work experience here so how about I take you under my wing and make it the best experience of your life?" asked Emma smiling.

Ava squealed with joy.

"Now was it you wanted to show me?" asked Emma.

Ava lead her over to a microscope with a piece of coral submerged in water under it. Emma looked through the microscope amazed. There in the coral was a small rare species of sea sponge.

"Ava, where did you find this?" asked Emma with amazement.

"Just on the beach earlier this morning" answered Ava.

"I have a dive in an hour. Would you like to come?" Emma asked Ava.

Ava's face lit up. Emma had never seen someone so happy.

"Meet me at the end of the jetty," said Emma.

Emma walked out of the lab grabbing her paperwork

and headed back to her old office. She began to pack up her things when Liam walked in.

"Hey sweetie, I don't have long. I have a dive to get too" explained Emma.

"Oh yeah sure, I'll come back later" replied Liam. "I love you, honey".

"I love you too," said Emma smiling.

She grabbed her diving gear and kissed Liam on her way out. There on the edge of the jetty was Ava waiting.

"Now Ava, for safety reasons I cannot let you dive but you can come on the boat. The water is that clear it will be like your swimming in the reef anyways" explained Emma.

"That's ok. I am still so excited" answered Ava.

Emma smiled down at her as they boarded the boat. Ava watched the island fade away as they head out into the sea. The boat came to a sudden stop.

"What's wrong?" asked Emma.

Emma took Ava's hand and lead her up to the deck. There in front of her in the distance was a pod of whales.

"Emma, they're humpback whales" squealed Ava.

Emma smiled down at her.

They sat on the deck and watched the whales swim off into the distance.

"I think we will just dive here today," said Emma.

Emma put on her diving gear with her team and went to dive in.

As Emma went to dive in first, she heard a scream from above.

"Emma!" screamed Ava.

Emma looked up and saw Ava pointing about a meter away from the boat. It was a reef shark.

"On second thoughts, let's go back to the lab" commanded Emma.

Emma walked back up to the deck and hugged Ava.

"Ava. You saved my life" said Emma gratefully.

Ava smiled up at Emma. She was truly her new idol. As the ship docked on the jetty, Emma thanked Ava once more. Emma walked back up to her office and started to box up her things. Tomorrow would be her first day as head researcher. As she finished boxing up her office, Liam walked in.

"What is going on here?" asked Liam

"I was going to tell you over dinner but I guess I could tell you now" explained Emma. "Sam promoted me to head researcher and I start tomorrow".

Liam stood in her doorway staring at her.

"Wow! Amazing honey! I am so proud of you" said Liam. "Like I was going to surprise propose to you now but this is way better"

"Hang on! What did you just say?" asked Emma

"Oh well, it is not a good as your promotion but" stared Liam as he bent down onto one knee. "Knowing you has been the best gift of my life. You are truly the best. I have always wanted a girl that was in it for the long run and now I have you. I love you so much. So, Emily Kate Smith, will you marry me?"

"Liam William Jones, I absolutely will marry you" replied Emma crying.

Liam put the ring on Emma's finger. It was beautiful, the diamond in the shell of a turtle. Emma leapt into his arms and did not let go.

"Would it be crazy if I have already made arrangements for us to be married tomorrow on Daydream Island?" asked Liam.

"It would be crazy! But I am so certain about this, let's do it. My first day can wait. I'm sure Sam will be happy to stick around for another day" replied Emma.

Emma and Liam walked over to Sam's office and told him everything. He understood and gave them his blessing. Tomorrow the research vessel would be waiting for them at the end of the jetty to take the to Daydream Island to get married.

Chapter 6

Today was the day Emma and Liam would vow to love each other forever. They were getting married. Emma had dreamed of getting married on Daydream Island, and today her dream will come true.

"Today is going to be full of surprises honey," said Liam.

"Really? What are these surprises?" asked Emma.

"Well, it would not be a surprise if I told you" replied Liam.

Emma rolled her eyes and walked into her closet holding a suit bag.

"What is that?" asked Liam.

"A surprise," said Emma laughing.

It was her wedding dress she had bought last year. Liam grabbed her hand as they walked down the jetty with their boat waiting. They watched Heron island fade into the distance as they approached Daydream Island. They were sailing in the open ocean, it glittered as bright as Emma's engagement ring diamond. The sun was at its peak shining onto the small island of Daydream. As they arrived at the jetty they were greeted by Emma's mother. Emma ran off the jetty and hugged her mom.

"What are you doing here mum?" asked Emma amazed.

"Well, I got a call yesterday from Liam saying someone was getting married so I thought I would come up to walk my beautiful daughter down the aisle" replied her mother. "And Liam, you're not meant to see the bride so I'll be taking over from here".

Emma's mother took her hand and lead her into her room.

"Right! You're getting married in an hour so it's time to fix this hair" said Lyn, Emma's mother.

Lyn curled and styled Emma's hair. As she finished, she placed a daisy crown on her hair. Emma walked into the bathroom and put on her wedding dress. It was beautiful. It was pale blue with lace sleeves. She looked at her reflection. She had never looked so beautiful. She walked out of the bathroom and Lyn started to cry.

"Mum. What's wrong?" asked Emma.

"My baby girl is all grown up, and you look beautiful. Liam is one lucky man" cried Lyn.

Emmer hugged her mum.

"Come on mum. It's time for me to get married" squealed Emma.

Lyn walked her daughter down to a set of stairs leading down to the beach. It was beautiful with an arch at the end of the aisle. Emma locked eyes with Liam and they both smiled. Liam had never seen anyone more beautiful. Emma took her mother's hand as she walked her down to Liam. At the end, Liam took her hand. The service started.

"Now I believe you have your own vows," said the marriage officiant.

Emma looked at Liam as she spoke.

"I remember the first time I saw you and I was like dam who is this. Even though it was only a year ago, this year has been the best year of my life. I love you with all my heart and I will love you forever. I cannot wait to spend the rest of my life with you" said Emma.

She took Liam's hand and placed his ring on his finger. Liam grabbed Emma's ring and started to speak.

"There is not much for me to say to you. I love you endlessly. You have turned my life upside down and blessed me every day. Every morning waking up next to you is a blessing in itself. I will love you for all eternity" said Liam.

He placed the ring on Emma's finger. They were now married. They had both gotten their dream job and both found the love of their lives. All was perfect.

Printed in the United States
By Bookmasters